LOUHI
WITCH OF NORTH FARM

LOUHI
WITCH OF NORTH FARM

A story from Finland's epic poem the Kalevala

RETOLD BY TONI DE GEREZ

PICTURES BY BARBARA COONEY

Viking Kestrel

It was snowing on Copper Mountain.
Louhi the Witch of North Farm stretched and scratched her back.

My! My! What shall I do today?

She sat down on her bony behind to think about it.

It was day and time to make some Witch plans.

She muttered and sputtered.
She grumbled and rumbled.

Shall I bake bread?
I could make blueberry soup.
I could go down and look at the boats.
Shall I start some new knitting?

But none of these plans suited her.
They were too everyday.

They were not good Witch plans.
Louhi felt like stirring up
some sort of trouble.
What good is a Witch who is too good?
Louhi scraped some frost off the window and looked out.

It was snowing softly.
The snow looked just right for skiing.
Not too wet. Not too icy.

Just enough crust for the skis to glide along smoothly.

So Louhi put on seven layers of clothes,
all on top of her nightshirt.
Then she pulled on her boots,
which were stuffed with good sweet grass.
Louhi took down her mittens, which had been drying by the hearth.

Her skis were waiting by the door.
Louhi liked to ski.
Of course, she could wish herself into a bird and fly.

She could wish herself into a fish and swim.

She could wish herself into a stone and roll down a hill.

But she felt like skiing
in the world so white, white.

Hei! Hei! I'm off!
she said to Nobody,
or perhaps to the Sit-behind-the-Stove, the quiet one.

There must be some Witch-Witch-Witchety things to do.

She glided smoothly over many meadows of dry heather
and over many low bushes.
Far away, far away from North Farm
across many lakes and rivers and hills.
And then Louhi changed her mind.

Up high into the air, into the sky,
into the snow clouds
Louhi skied.

This is the real way to ski, said Louhi.

Suddenly Louhi stopped.
She could hear music.
She looked down.

It must be Vainamoinen.
Only Vainamoinen could make music like that.

Vainamoinen was known all over the world,
in all Four Corners.

He was the Great Singer.
He was the Great Boat Maker.

Why, if he felt like it, he could sing a boat together
with only his magic words!

And he was the Great Knower.
He knew about everything Over and Under and Up and Down.

Louhi skied down a cloud-hill
and hid behind a chokecherry bush.

There he was!
Vainamoinen was sitting on a stone.
His harp was laid out flat across his knees.
He drew his fingers gently across the strings
and the tones leaped into melody.

Vainamoinen played.
Never before had there been such sweetness of sound.
Birds came flocking to his shoulders.
Fish came to the lake shore among the reeds.

The pine trees made merry.
Some old tree stumps hopped about as though they were young again.

All the animals in the forest pricked up their ears
and came running,
the deer, the foxes, the wolves.

The Seven Stars of the Great Bear came circling down
from the sky.

Vainamoinen played on and on.
Even the sun and the moon wanted to come close.

The white moon stepped out of the sky
and settled upon a birch bough.

The yellow sun came to rest upon a pine branch.

The music was so sweet.
Not a single leaf moved. Not a pine cone dropped.

All was still except for Vainamoinen and his music.

Suddenly Louhi the Witch
came out from behind the chokecherry bush.
Louhi made a double somersault over the bush.

And Louhi turned into an eagle.

Then, screaming and shaking with mean laughter,
Louhi flew to the top of the birch tree.
Louhi stole the moon!

Louhi flew to the pine tree.
Louhi stole the sun!

Off she flew with the sun and the moon.
Louhi flew back to her North Farm.

Then what did Louhi do?
Louhi hid the moon and the sun
behind nine great locks, behind nine great doors
in her storeroom in Copper Mountain.

She almost forgot to turn herself back into Louhi, but
she turned another double somersault backwards—

And there was Witch Louhi,
the toothless one, except for one old back tooth.

Louhi pulled up her stockings.

She said, Now for a little bowl of porridge!
Where is my dear little porridge spoon?
And the porridge spoon jumped on top of the table.

Now it was dark everywhere.
The land was plunged into terrible darkness.
The people and wood creatures could not find their way home.

Darkness was everywhere, dark, dark darkness.
The wind howled angrily through the cold dark sky.

Nobody knew whether it was morning or evening.

Musti, the black dog, rolled up into a black, shivering ball.

Muurikki, the black and white cow,
bumped around in her shed.

The black door did not know inside from outside.

Black smoke rising from the roof-hole asked,
Shall I blow North or South?
It is all the same. Nothing but dark.

Something had to be done.
Everybody had worry on their faces.

Vainamoinen went to find his friend Seppo, the smith.

Seppo was a great smith.
He had forged the Sampo, hadn't he, the magic chest?

Surely he could make a silver moon.
He could make a golden sun.
And the earth would be happy again.

Seppo, the smith, worked hard.
At last he forged a beautiful moon.
He forged a beautiful golden sun.

He climbed the pine tree and placed the new sun on a top branch.
He climbed the birch tree and placed the new moon there.

Nothing happened.
There was no light.
Darkness still covered the earth with a heavy blanket.

Seppo became very angry.
I shall make an iron collar and nine terrible iron chains
to wrap around the neck of a certain Witch!

CLANG, CLANG, was the noise in his forge
as he made the nine terrible iron chains and the iron collar.

Vainamoinen, in the meanwhile,
went off to Copper Mountain to try to find the sun and the moon.

Vainamoinen crossed mountains and rivers.

At last he was near Copper Mountain.
Louhi's dogs barked and growled.

Louhi listened through the moss between the logs
and peeked through a hole in the wall.

Louhi opened the door a crack.

She screamed, "The sun and the moon are here!
But they are mine forever. Go away!"

And she shook her Nameless Finger at him,
the most powerful of all fingers!

Vainamoinen went back home sadly, across marshes and rivers.

But Louhi was curious.
What were they up to now, those two,
Vainamoinen and Seppo?

I'll just fly over and find out, said Louhi.
Louhi changed herself into a hawk.
She flew from her North Farm to Kaleva.

She perched on top of Seppo's door
and asked in a pretty little voice,
"What are you making, Seppo?"

He stopped his pounding for a moment.

He said, "I am making an iron collar
and nine terrible iron chains
to wrap around the skinny gray neck of a certain Witch!"

"But why are you going to do that?" asked Louhi in a
soft, sweet, little voice.
"And who is the Witch, if I may ask?"

"She is the Witch who stole our sun
and who stole our moon."

A big stone of fear dropped into the heart of Louhi.

Quickly she flew back to her Copper Mountain, to her North Farm.

She took her nine iron keys and opened
the nine iron doors of her storeroom.

There were the sun and the moon.
They were sitting sadly side by side.

Louhi picked them up in her arms.
She flew back high over the marshes and the sea.

She placed the sun back in the pine tree.
She placed the moon back in the birch.

With another of her somersault tricks Louhi became a dove.
She flew to the top of the door of Seppo's forge.

"What do you wish, little dove?" asked Seppo.

"Just to tell you
the moon and the sun are back.
Look! Look!"

Now there would be time:
Night time and daytime.
There would be weather:
Winter with ice and snow and cold winds.
Summer with bright-eyed flowers, birds,
and tall grasses.

The sun and the moon are back.
Look! Listen!
Louhi has flown back to her home
in the North Farm.
And Vainamoinen is singing again.

AUTHOR'S NOTE

Thousands of years ago in Finland, that faraway northern land, stories were told from generation to generation, sung through the long winter nights around the fire, at festivals, or on fishing or hunting expeditions. The stories told of the creation of the world at the beginning of time, of ancient heroes, of the cycle of nature, of beliefs and magic rituals, of strange and mighty spells.

A little more than a century ago, Elias Lönnrot, a traveling doctor, gathered these songs from the "song villages," mainly along the Karelian-Russian border, and from this oral poetry the Finnish national epic, the *Kalevala*, was born.

Louhi, Witch of North Farm, a tale taken from the *Kalevala*, tells of the struggle of light and dark, the need for order in the primeval world, what happens when it is disturbed, and how Vainemoinen the Knower and Seppo the Smith carry out their cosmic task of returning the sun and moon to their planetary duties.

The narrative for the original prologue to the *Kalevala* begins:

"Now the cold told a tale to me
The rain dictated poems
Another tale the winds brought
The birds added words
The treetops speeches…"

And now I begin my tale.

T. de G.

The artwork for *Louhi, Witch of North Farm*, was painted on Strathmore illustration board which was coated four times with acrylic gesso, and each coat was sanded with fine sandpaper. The artist used acrylic paints with Prismacolor and Derwent colored pencils and some pastel chalk.

VIKING KESTREL

Viking Penguin Inc., 40 West 23rd Street, New York, New York 10010, U.S.A.
Penguin Books Ltd., Harmondsworth, Middlesex, England
Penguin Books Australia Ltd., Ringwood, Victoria, Australia
Penguin Books Canada Limited, 2801 John Street, Markham, Ontario, Canada L3R 1B4
Penguin Books (N.Z.) Ltd., 182–190 Wairau Road, Auckland 10, New Zealand

Text copyright © Toni de Gerez, 1986
Illustrations copyright © Barbara Cooney Porter, 1986
All rights reserved

First published in 1986 by Viking Penguin Inc.
Published simultaneously in Canada

LIBRARY OF CONGRESS CATALOGING IN PUBLICATION DATA
De Gerez, Toni.   Louhi, Witch of North Farm.
Summary: Louhi's plan to steal the sun and the moon
backfires when the gods learn of her mischievous scheme.
[1. Folklore—Finland]   I. Cooney, Barbara, ill.   II. Title.
PZ8.1.D35Lo 1986   398.2'2'094897 [E]   84-21600   ISBN 0-670-80556-4
Separations produced in Hong Kong by Imago Publishing, Ltd
Manufactured in U.S.A. by Lake Book Cuneo, Melrose Park, IL
     2   3   4   5   90   89   88   87
Set in Optima

For Marja Leena Rautalin
and the Finnish Literature Society, Helsinki
T. de G.

For dear Phoebe
B.C.